Holiday Hullabaloo

For Poppy Isabella Frances Griffin-Bent
and special thanks to Daisy

FELICITY WISHES

Felicity Wishes © 2000 Emma Thomson
Licensed by White Lion Publishing

Text and Illustrations © 2007 Emma Thomson

First published in Great Britain in 2007 by Hodder Children's Books

A Catalogue record for this book is available from the British Library.

ISBN: 978 0 340 94397 7

Printed and bound in Hong Kong by Sheck Wah Tong Printing Press Ltd.

The paper and board used in this paperback by Hodder Children's Books are natural recyclable
products made from wood grown in sustainable forests. The manufacturing processes
conform to the environmental regulations of the country of origin.

Hodder Children's Books
A division of Hachette Children's Books, 338 Euston Road, London NW1 3BH

Emma Thomson's

felicity Wishes®

Holiday Hullabaloo

and other stories

Hodder
Children's
Books

A division of Hachette Children's Books

How to make your Felicity wishes

W I S H

With this book comes an extra-special wish
for you and your best friend.
Hold the book together at each end and
both close your eyes.
Wriggle your noses and think of a
number under ten.
Open your eyes, whisper the numbers you
thought of to each other.
Add these numbers together. This is your

Magic Number.

you

best
friend

Place your little finger
on the stars, and say your magic number
out loud together. Now make your wish
quietly to yourselves. And maybe, one day,
your wish might just come true.

Love felicity x

CONTENTS

Sailing Success

Sailing Success

Felicity Wishes and her best friends Holly, Polly and Daisy were all sitting round Winnie's coffee table, trying to decide where to go on their summer holiday. Winnie's living room was crammed with shelves full of souvenirs, gathered from every place she had ever visited in Fairy World.

"I always bring something home with me to remember my trip," Winnie explained to her friends. "I've got all sorts of things from all sorts of places!"

 13

Felicity looked in awe at the wonderful collection. Winnie had statues from Everycolour Lake, shells from Glitter Beach, bottles from Fizzy Pop Stream, rocks from Lookgood National Park and dolls from Sew and Mend Valley. Felicity had read all about these magical locations in geography class, but even in her wildest dreams she had never visited so many exotic places.

"This year I want to bring back something extra special, unlike anything I've collected before!" Winnie said dreamily. "It will be my prize souvenir."

"Yes, but where are we going to go?" Polly asked desperately. "You've been everywhere in Fairy World!"

The fairies pored through the pages of holiday brochures, but no one could decide where to go. Every time someone suggested a place, it was considered too far, too boring or too energetic by the others. After several hours, the fairies gave up and went home without having decided a thing!

The next day as the fairy friends flew along the High Street in Little Blossoming, Winnie stopped outside Travel Tactics, the travel agents.

"Look!" she shouted, pointing her wand at an advert in the shop window.

Why not relax in style and have a wonderful adventure at the same time?

Be part of a stylish yacht crew and explore the waters of Fairy World.

Join the Jolly Sparkle and have the holiday of a lifetime!

"Wow!" said Winnie, almost bursting with excitement. "That sounds like the most perfect holiday in the world."

Felicity looked at the other fairies, aghast. A sailing trip wasn't exactly the relaxing beach holiday she had in mind. But Felicity didn't want to shatter her friend's dream, so she remained silent as Winnie fluttered inside, dragging the other fairies with her.

"Hello!" she said excitedly to the travel agent fairy. "I'd like to book the boating holiday in your window… for five fairies!"

Winnie had known at once that the holiday was the one for her and she was sure that her friends would enjoy it too…

* * *

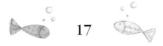

Felicity, however, was not so confident! As she packed her suitcase a few days later she just didn't know what to take – flip-flops or pumps, water wings or micro-light wings, swimming costume or waterproofs? She had never been on a boating holiday and had no idea what to expect. In her hearts of hearts, she wasn't even sure she wanted to go.

Holly was also having second thoughts. She was worried that her hair would go frizzy in the salty sea air.

Daisy was already panicking about leaving her precious flowers for such a long time. And Polly felt guilty about missing three whole weeks of Tooth Fairy night classes.

But Winnie was excited enough for all the fairies and couldn't wait until they took to the open ocean!

* * *

The morning of the big holiday arrived and the friends all flew together to the harbour. As they drew closer, they could see their boat bobbing about in the water, waiting for them to board. It was gleaming and the sails were dazzlingly bright.

 19

"Wow!" said Felicity, landing with a fairy-like bump. "I didn't expect the boat to be so sparkling! It looks magical!"

Standing beside the boat were two fairies. The fairy on the left looked very neat and tidy, quite like Polly with her short, silky dark hair. But the other fairy was slightly more conspicuous! Her clothes were faded as though they had been left in the sun for years, her shoes had holes in them where the toes were worn through, and her frizzy, almost white hair stood out on end, as though she was hanging upside down!

The most peculiar thing though was that she kept swaying; even when the fairies introduced themselves and shook her hand, she continued to

 20

sway gently to and fro as if she was on board a ship in rough seas!

"Hi there, I'm Sandy," she said as she shook Felicity's hand. "You'll have to excuse me, I've got on-land-swayitus! The doctor said that I spend so much time on boats that I can't tell the difference between land and water, and my body keeps swaying no matter where I am! I've got some potion which helps, but I can't spend too much time on land or I start to feel land-sick!"

Felicity stifled a giggle.

The other fairy introduced herself as Ginny in a very quiet, shy voice. "I'm a trainee wildlife fairy," she whispered, "and I have to spend three weeks on a boat studying the seas of Fairy World. I can't wait to see some

of the amazing sea creatures but, well, I'm a little nervous… I've never been on a boat before."

"Don't worry," said Felicity, putting an arm around her new friend. "We haven't spent much time on boats either. It'll be fun!" she said, trying to convince herself as much as Ginny.

"Come on!" Sandy interrupted loudly. "Let's set sail!"

The fairies picked up their bags and hurried after Sandy, climbing the steep plank on to the deck of the boat.

"OK, listen up. I'm going to show you all around, then we'll get going," said Sandy. "At the moment the wind is quite strong so we'll only use the sail, but as it drops we'll use the engine as well."

While Sandy was speaking, Polly was

rummaging in her bag. She produced
a notebook and pen and started
furiously taking notes on everything
Sandy was saying.

Felicity tried hard to concentrate,
but she found Sandy's hair very
distracting!

"Right, follow me!" Sandy called

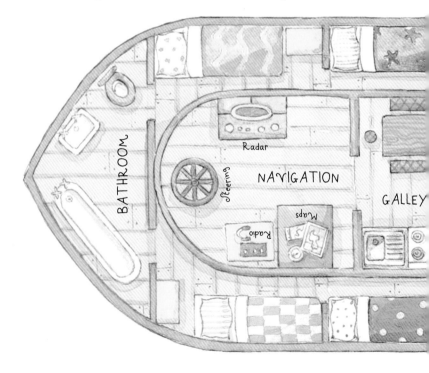

BATHROOM

Radar

Steering

NAVIGATION

GALLEY

Maps

Radio

over her shoulder. She took the fairies round the whole boat, from top to bottom. She showed them everything on the deck, including the wheel with which she would steer the boat, the sail and the winches used to raise and lower it, the boom, holding the bottom of the sail taut and, most

importantly, the locker where the life rafts belonged.

Below deck, Felicity and her friends saw the galley, the navigation area and their cabins, each containing fairy bunk beds.

As Felicity fluttered up to her top bunk and started to unpack, she suddenly realized that life on board a boat might be rather exciting after all...

* * *

By the time the fairy friends had resurfaced, Sandy had taken up the anchor and the boat was sailing out of harbour into the blue ocean.

"Excuse me, can I ask a question?" Polly asked once they were safely out of the harbour.

"Yes, of course!" Sandy answered.

"Well, you've shown us where we'll be sleeping, but where do you sleep?" Polly enquired.

"Oh, I don't!" Sandy said breezily.

"You don't sleep at all?" Polly asked,

shocked at Sandy's response.

"No, I don't need to sleep. The sea air keeps me wide awake!" she explained.

Polly frowned. Surely every fairy had to sleep some time! But before she had a chance to say anything else, Sandy was giving instructions to everyone.

"OK," she called to the fairies, "there are hundreds of jobs to do and we're going to take it in turns doing them all. As you are not yet familiar with the boat, I will be the helmsfairy today."

Felicity looked quizzically at Ginny.

"That's the fairy who steers the boat," Ginny whispered. "I researched how boats work at the library, before the trip."

Felicity smiled. She must remember to tell Polly that Ginny had been doing research too. Polly had spent the last two days in the library finding out as much as she could about boats. Felicity was sure they would all become the best of friends.

"So, for today I want Winnie to be based in the navigation area," Sandy continued. "Winnie, you will study the maps and decide the course we will take. The sea is your oyster so take us wherever your heart wants to go."

Winnie, with her adventurous streak, was very happy about that.

"Holly and Daisy, I want you two to work the mainsail. I will be here to tell you what to do. Polly, you can organize the living quarters and

generally maintain the working positions aboard the boat. Felicity and Ginny, you are in charge of the telescope. You will need to take it in turns watching the open water and looking out for any obstacles that may get in our way. OK, everyone to their positions!"

Felicity and Ginny hurried to the bow of the boat, the narrow front end where Sandy had shown them the telescope earlier.

"I'm so excited! I can't wait to see the sea life out here, it's supposed to be amazing!" Ginny enthused.

Felicity was just as excited about making a new friend! She couldn't wait to ask Ginny where she came from and what her hobbies were. For Felicity, making new friends was

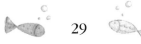

always the best thing about going on holiday.

* * *

For the next few days Felicity and Ginny, Holly and Daisy, and Winnie and Polly all took it in turns doing the various chores on the boat. In between they scrubbed the deck, cooked meals (all except Felicity, whose cooking might have given them seasickness!), studied their navigation books and, at the end of a long day, fell to sleep in their tiny cabins.

It wasn't the holiday any of them had imagined – especially for Felicity. She had dreamt about sunbathing whilst drinking fruit cocktails, and watching dolphins rise out of the sea as a brilliant-orange sun dipped into

the water at the
end of each day.
But life on board
a boat was so
busy that Felicity
didn't even have
time to pick up her
copy of *Fairy Girl*
once! And Holly's
worst fear had been
realized when her
hair went from
frizzy to nest-like
in a matter of
days! Polly was
fed up of
cleaning the
other fairies'
mess, and
even Winnie

wasn't having
as much fun
as she had
expected.
Her
adventuring
heart felt
trapped on
the boat and
she started to
worry that she
would never find
her dream souvenir
to take home.

* * *

"Oh, if only something exciting would happen," Felicity sighed to Ginny as they sat in the bow, taking it in turns to look through the telescope for the hundredth time!

 32

"I know," Ginny agreed. "I haven't seen any tropical birds or fish, and the water is so calm we don't even seem to be moving!"

Then, all of a sudden and as if by magic, something caught the corner of Felicity's eye. Something was bobbing up and down on the surface of the water.

"Look! What's that?" she said to Ginny, shocked to see anything breaking the endless clear blue water.

"I can't see anything," said Ginny, looking all around her.

"There, look!" Felicity came away from the telescope so Ginny could see.

Ginny squealed. "Oh! Well, yes, it looks like a bottle. And it's got something in it!"

 33

Felicity called the others to come and have a look.

"It could be a message from lost fairies at sea!" said Daisy excitedly.

"Or it could be hundreds of years old," said Polly. "Maybe it's a time capsule from fairies long ago!"

"Or maybe it's filled with age-matured magic juice!" mused Holly.

"Whatever it is, we had better try and get it quick before it floats away!" said Sandy, fluttering off to steer the boat towards the bottle.

Polly went to get the fishing net she had seen stowed away on deck during her supply check a few days before, whilst Felicity kept a close eye on the bottle. It wasn't long before the yacht was floating alongside it.

 34

"OK, one of us needs to lean overboard with the fishing net while the others hold on to her feet. There is no time to get water wings so whatever we do we mustn't fall in!" Sandy commanded.

"I'll do it!" Felicity volunteered, feeling much braver than usual. Carefully taking the fishing net, she leant over the side of the boat and Winnie grabbed hold of her toes.

"Oh, no, it's no use. I'm nowhere near," she said, dropping the net on deck.

"Polly, hold Winnie's feet and Holly, hold Polly's feet so we can form a chain to reach it!" Ginny suggested.

The fairies did as Ginny said, and they came closer to the bottle, but still they couldn't quite catch it.

 35

"Just a tiny bit more!" Felicity called, hovering above the water.

Ginny held on to Holly's feet and Daisy held on to Ginny's, and before they knew it Felicity was cheering!

"I've got it, I've got it!" she called from the front of the line. "Pull me in!"

Each fairy pulled the fairy in front until they all bumped back on deck in a heap.

Felicity pulled the stopper out of the bottle and peered inside.

"It's not juice…" she muttered. "And it's not a time capsule…" she teased.

"What is it? What is it?" the fairies surrounding her demanded.

"It's nothing!" she said, handing it to Winnie. "Just a weather-worn label that's fallen off inside."

Winnie shook the bottle and the

rolled-up paper label fell out.

"Well, at one point it was age-matured magic juice!" said Winnie, opening it out to read.

Holly, Polly, Felicity, Sandy and Ginny suddenly looked startled.

"What?" said Winnie, noting the surprise on their faces. "It was! Look, it says here: 'Age-matured Magic Juice, 1771'. A vintage year, by the looks of things; not a drop left!"

Still the other fairies said nothing, but stared mesmerized at the label.

"Look on the other side!" murmured Felicity to Winnie.

Winnie turned the label over to see what they had all been staring at. "Oh, my goodness!" she burst out.

On the reverse of the magic juice label was the most beautiful and

intricate pattern she had ever seen.
Gold and blue swirls, bright-orange
glistening fish,
delicately painted
palm trees and
glistening golden
areas made it one
of the most amazing
things Winnie had
ever seen.

"Who in Fairy
World would
have spent so much time painting
such a beautiful pattern on the back
of a bottle label?" asked Winnie.

"Maybe we'll never know," said
Felicity, gently stroking the label's
edges. But whatever happens, we've
found your extra-special holiday
souvenir!"

As Felicity lay in bed that night, she couldn't help wondering about the picture. She had a feeling that it was going to lead them to the best holiday of their lives!

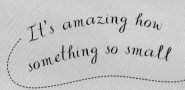

It's amazing how
something so small

can lead to
something so big.

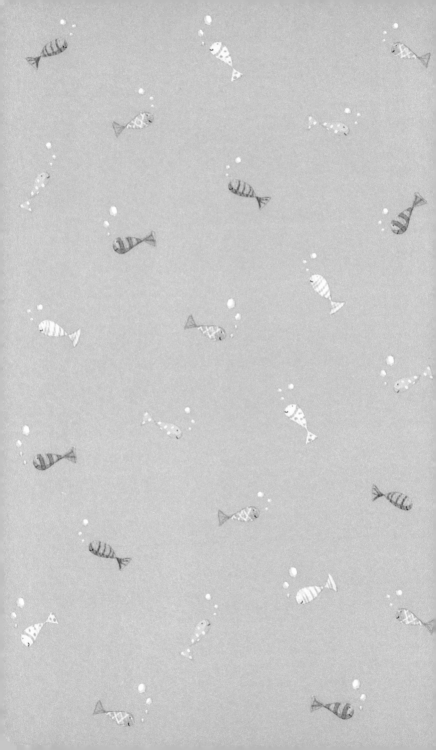

Mystery Message

Mystery Message

Felicity Wishes and her friends had
decided to go on a boating holiday,
but it had not quite been what the
fairies had hoped for. Life on board
the boat was very busy. Felicity had
wanted a relaxing holiday reading
her copy of *Fairy Girl* from cover to
cover, but so far she'd barely had
time to pick it up.

Then, a week into their trip, the
fairies had spotted a bottle floating
on the sea. After struggling to reach it,

they'd discovered a beautiful picture inside.

Winnie had thought it would make a wonderful souvenir to take home. But Felicity couldn't stop wondering at the picture's intricate detail.

"It just doesn't make sense," she said over breakfast one morning. "Why would anyone draw such a beautiful thing only to put it in a bottle and send it out to sea?"

"Perhaps," Daisy was thinking out loud, "they put the picture in the bottle for safe-keeping and then the boat they were on got caught in a storm and the bottle was thrown overboard."

The fairies all looked at Daisy, marvelling at her elaborate imagination.

"I think it must be some kind of message," Felicity said. "There must be something hidden in that picture that the fairy who drew it wanted other fairies to know."

Polly had been very quiet during breakfast, staring into space, quite unlike her usual self.

"What's wrong, Polly?" asked Ginny. Felicity and her friends had met Ginny on the boat. She was training to be a wildlife fairy and had to spend three weeks at sea, learning about the sea life in Fairy World. So far she hadn't seen anything!

"Oh, nothing," Polly replied. "I was just thinking how quiet Sandy has been since we found the bottle."

"It could be because she hasn't slept since we got on board!" suggested Holly. Sandy, the Skipper Fairy in charge of the boat, claimed she didn't need to sleep.

"Yes, I suppose that must be it," agreed Polly.

* * *

Sandy remained pensive all day, hardly muttering a word to any of the fairies.

That evening, as the fairies gathered at the table for supper, chatting about nothing in particular, Sandy fluttered up to them.

"Hu-hum," she coughed, clearing her throat. "I can't keep this to myself any longer!" she blurted. "I know what the

picture means – but it's a secret and I really shouldn't be telling you."

The fairies looked at her in wonder.

"You can tell us!" said Felicity. "We keep secrets for each other all the time – we won't tell anyone."

The other fairies agreed.

"Well, that's what I thought," continued Sandy, "and you probably would have worked it out sooner or later anyway."

The fairies were on the edges of their seats, their wings quivering in anticipation.

"The truth is... the picture is... a map," Sandy revealed.

"I knew it!" said Felicity. "I had a feeling it was more than just a picture! Where does the map lead to?"

"It leads to Wing Island," Sandy replied.

"Wing Island?" Polly exclaimed. "No such place exists!" Polly was the cleverest of all the fairies and was brilliant at geography; she knew the map of Fairy World back to front.

"Yes, it does," Sandy almost

whispered. "It's a very well-kept secret. I only know because I used to work in a wing factory. Wing Island is where wings come from."

Daisy, who had been closest to the edge of her seat, toppled right off and clattered to the floor in her surprise.

"But I thought wings were actually made in a wing-making factory," Holly said.

"That's what you're supposed to think," Sandy explained, "but the wing factory is just a front. If everyone knew they were made on Wing Island, it would be overrun with fairies wanting new wings."

"But who makes the wings on Wing Island?" Ginny asked.

"No one does," Sandy replied. "It's magic. They all fly from the island to

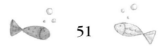

the factory, and the flight is a crucial part of their forming process. If they get disrupted, they don't make it as proper wings."

"Well, let's go there!" Winnie said excitedly. "Now we know about it, we have to go and see it. It'll be the adventure of a lifetime! How do we get there, Sandy?"

"I have no idea, and the map is a mystery to me. I just recognized the wing-shaped island in the middle."

The fairies all looked at the map. The brown shape in the middle, spotted with sparkly green palm trees and outlined with glittering gold, was indeed the shape of a pair of wings. Surrounding it were blue and silver swirls with glittering golden dots on them, bright-orange glistening fish,

and a red splodge with two black dots like eyes. But there were no instructions, and they didn't recognize anywhere on the map.

"Oh well, I suppose it'll have to remain a mystery," Winnie said disappointedly, her wings drooping so much they almost touched the deck.

"It's still a beautiful picture though," said Felicity, trying to cheer her

friend up. "It will look great on your souvenir shelf, Winnie."

Just then, as the fairies sat pondering the map, the boat jumped and shuddered as though it had collided with something very big.

"Oh!" screamed Holly, clutching at her glass of strawberry milkshake as it tipped over on the table and into her lap.

"What was that?" Polly called over to Sandy, who had fluttered to the wheel to try and steady the boat.

"I have no idea," Sandy called back, looking at the sea on all sides. "It felt like we hit a rock, but I can't see anything."

Felicity and her friends scrambled around the table, picking up their cutlery and plates from the deck.

"Well, I hope it doesn't happen again," Daisy said, rather scared.

"At least nothing got spilt on the map," sighed Winnie, who had luckily been holding the map in her hands. "There's always a tiny chance we could find the island. Let's have another look at it tomorrow."

With that the fairies finished clearing up and went to bed, exhausted after

another day on board. Sandy settled down on lookout for the night.

✳ ✳ ✳

The next day, Felicity woke much earlier than usual. Peering out of the tiny porthole next to her bunk bed she saw that it was barely sunrise. "That's strange," she thought to herself, "I wonder why I've woken up so early."

Just then the boat jumped a little, just as it had done the night before at supper.

"Oh!" Felicity exclaimed, sitting up and almost banging her head on the roof of her tiny cabin. Again the boat swayed and Felicity clambered over the side of her bed and down the ladder to the bottom bunk where Ginny was fast asleep.

"Wake up!" Felicity said in Ginny's

ear, poking her with her wand.

Ginny opened her eyes blearily.
"Huh? What's wrong?" she groaned.

"I think we've hit something again!"
Felicity cried, just as the boat rocked
again.

Ginny scrambled out of bed and
followed Felicity as she hurried into
the corridor. Polly and Winnie were
coming out of their room and Daisy
and Holly were emerging out of theirs.
They all exchanged worried glances
as they rushed up on deck.

Once there, they couldn't believe
their eyes. Alongside the boat was a
huge, bright-red octopus! One
tentacle was draped over the deck of
the boat, hitting the floor repeatedly,
right next to where Sandy was lying
unconscious!

"Get away from her, you big meany!"
cried Felicity, charging towards the
giant beast.

The octopus immediately recoiled
his tentacle. The other fairies stood
as still as statues, their faces drained
of colour and their wings shaking
uncontrollably. That is, all except

Ginny, who had the biggest grin ever spread across her face.

"What's s-so f-f-funny, G-G-G-Ginny?" Felicity stuttered.

"It's an octogiant!" Ginny squealed excitedly. "I never thought I'd be lucky enough to see one of these!"

The fairies all stared at her in wonder, except Sandy who was still lying on the deck and had started to snore very loudly.

"A what?" asked Polly.

"An octogiant! They're the most friendly sea creatures in Fairy World, and the biggest."

"So it wasn't trying to squash Sandy then?" asked Felicity, slightly embarrassed.

"Oh no, it would never do that. I expect she fainted when she saw it and now she's fallen into a deep sleep." Ginny suggested. "After all, she hasn't slept for ages!"

Felicity, Polly and Holly carefully picked Sandy up and placed her in a hammock, where she continued to snore gently.

Meanwhile, Ginny rushed over to the side of the boat, where the octogiant was solemnly watching the fairies. She started waving her arms up and down,

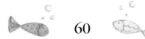

first her right then her left, repeating the move over and over.

"Greetings!" she called out to him. "And apologies! My friend probably fainted because she thought you were a monster, but I know you're not!"

The octogiant went from looking as though he was about to cry to looking like the happiest creature on the planet. Then he started waving his eight tentacles about in huge arches.

"What's he doing, Ginny?" Winnie called.

"He's talking to me!" Ginny replied, stifling a giggle. "He says it happens all the time. Fairies see him and faint, then he tries to wake them up but they faint again as soon as they open their eyes! He never knows what to do!"

The fairies all looked at Ginny in wonder.

"Come over!" Ginny called to them, but they were a little reluctant to move.

Felicity took a deep breath and walked over to the octogiant.

"I'm Ginny, and this is my friend Felicity," Ginny told the great creature, waving her arms above her head.

The octogiant lifted one of his huge

tentacles out of the water and on to the side of the boat, where Felicity shook it with her outstretched hand. She noticed that he wasn't using all his tentacles. One of them seemed to be caught on the boat's rudder.

"Look! We've got to help him!" she cried, pointing at the trapped tentacle. Felicity and the other fairies ran to the rudder and pulled and pulled with all their might until they managed to untangle the octogiant from the boat.

"He says thank you!" Ginny cried. "He was worried he was never going to get away. He says his name is Ollie and he's very pleased to meet all of us. He has swum in these waters for years, but has never come across anyone as friendly as us! "

Suddenly, Felicity had an idea.

"Do you think he knows how to get to Wing Island?"

"Oh, good idea!" cried Winnie. She rushed below deck and came back with the picture from the bottle in her hand.

Ginny continued to wave her arms about as the octogiant looked at the map and began to wave his tentacles again.

"He knows where it is and he'd like to help us get there!" said Ginny, jumping up and down in excitement.

Felicity and her friends whooped and cheered. One by one, the fairies ventured forward to greet Ollie.

Ginny translated what Ollie was saying, explaining that the pretty golden dots in the blue and silver swirls were actually wing-shaped

rocks, jutting out from the sea. The first was not far away at all, and from there each rock got bigger and bigger, until at last they led to the island itself.

Taking her compass out of her pocket, Winnie worked out which direction they would have to sail in to begin their voyage.

"Thank you so much," Felicity said to Ollie. Ginny laughed, waving her arms at him. Ollie waved six of his tentacles as he floated away from the boat, one to each of the fairies.

"Oh dear," said Polly, turning away from the sea.

"What is it?" asked Holly.

"Well, how are we going to get there if Sandy doesn't wake up?" Polly said worriedly, pointing her wand at

Sandy, who was still fast asleep.

Winnie smiled. "I've been watching Sandy all week," she said. "I think I can steer the boat!" And with that she rushed to the wheel.

It took the fairies hours to find the first wing-shaped rock, but once they did, their cheers could be heard for miles around! After that each rock became bigger, as Ollie had said, until at last they glimpsed the shimmering outline of land along the horizon. The closer they got, the more and more magical Wing Island looked.

Polly had spent the journey packing a dinghy full of the fairies' belongings and food, ready for their stay on the island.

As the sun was setting over the sea, Sandy finally woke up.

 66

"Where am I?" she said, rubbing her head.

"Next stop, Wing Island!" Winnie called from her place behind the wheel.

Sandy was immediately on her toes and fluttering over to Winnie.

"Goodness! How did you find it?" she asked, gazing at the island as they drew closer.

"You'd still think you were dreaming if I told you," Felicity replied.

"If only I could go on land," Sandy sighed.

"Why can't you?" Felicity asked.

"My on-land-swayitus, remember," Sandy said.

Since being on board the swaying ship, the fairies had forgotten that Sandy had a condition called on-land-swayitus. She had spent so much time at sea that if she went on land she continued to sway to an alarming extent.

The fairies all agreed that while

 68

they were exploring the island Sandy and Ginny would go back to Little Blossoming and get more potion, then they would return to collect them in a week.

As the sun went down, the fairies got closer and closer to the island.

"Wow!" they exclaimed together. There were hundreds of pairs of wings floating through the air, fluttering all around the island, rising up from the very middle. Each pair was a different size and shape, and set against the pink sunset sky they looked simply beautiful. The beaches had purely golden waves of sand, and tall green palm trees edged the forest in the middle.

"It's just so perfect," said Daisy, mesmerized by the island's beauty.

"I want to stay here for ever!" said Felicity dreamily.

The whole island seemed to give off a sparkling radiance.

As they said goodbye to Sandy and Ginny, and lowered their dinghy over the side of the yacht they couldn't wait to begin the magical adventures they all knew they would have on Wing Island.

Everything will always be fine

with good friends by your side.

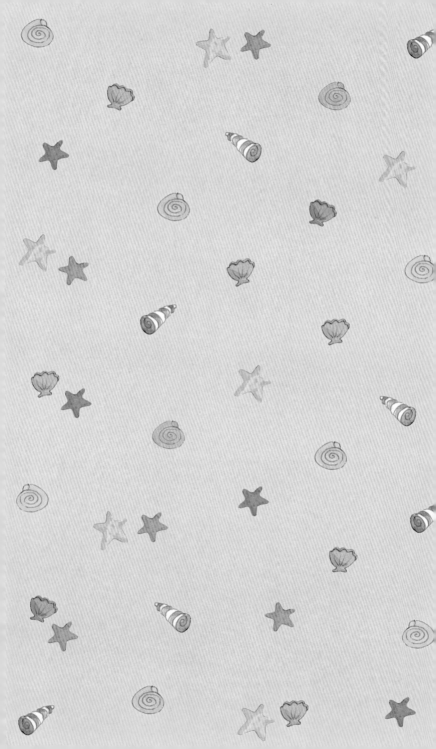

Holiday Hullabaloo

Holiday Hullabaloo

"It's wonderful!" Felicity Wishes shouted, doing a loop-the-loop in the air as she fluttered out of the bright-yellow dinghy and landed on Wing Island.

Polly, Holly, Daisy and Winnie followed her, staring wide-eyed at the brilliant-white sands that stretched for miles around and the green jungle glistening in the distance. They had discovered Wing Island only by magical chance, when a beautiful

map floating in a bottle showed them the way.

As the friends looked around, they noticed that they were the only fairies in this very special place.

Sandy, the Skipper Fairy on the boat that had brought them here, had told the fairies a great secret: contrary to fairy folktale, wings are not made in factories, but on Wing Island. From there, the wings fly to factories all over Fairy World, where they are sorted and packaged ready for fairies to wear.

As far as the fairies' eyes could see, wings were fluttering up from the heart of the deep jungle and heading out to sea in all different directions.

The friends gazed in awe, wondering where exactly the wings were coming from.

"I can't wait to explore the island!" announced Winnie excitedly, already trying to work out the best route into the jungle.

Felicity giggled at her adventurous friend. After such a long, hard day all she wanted to do was rest on the soft sand.

* * *

By the time the fairies had unpacked their bags, put up their tents and lit a campfire, the sky had turned from blue to black. For a while they sat cosily around the fire, drinking hot chocolate – but they

 80

were so tired after their long journey
that it wasn't long before they were
snuggled up in their tents, snoring
softly.

The fairies spent the next day
having fun on the beach – reading
magazines, playing catch with

coconuts, swimming in the crystal-
clear sea, staring up at the cloudless
blue sky, and finally snuggling round
the campfire, telling funny stories

and cooking marshmallows until the night stars twinkled bright.

That night, just past midnight when all the fairies were fast asleep, the ground suddenly began to shake. It was only very slightly at first, but then it built up into a low, rumbling sound that escalated into a huge growling noise.

"What was that?" Felicity whispered, sitting up in her sleeping bag.

"I haven't a clue!" said Polly, rubbing her eyes. She could hear a whooshing noise, followed by a very loud buzzing.

Felicity and Polly nudged Holly, but she was sound asleep, completely unaware that anything was happening. Together, the two friends slowly unzipped the tent and peeped their heads outside, but it was so dark they

 82

couldn't see a thing. Winnie and Daisy were still asleep in their tent.

"Hmmm," said Felicity, puzzled. "I suppose we'll just have to investigate in the morning."

* * *

"I've never heard anything like it!" Felicity told Daisy, Holly and Winnie at breakfast the next morning as she described the noises from the previous night.

"It sounds like a tropical storm to me," Winnie suggested.

"Hmm. Maybe that explains why there weren't any wings in the sky yesterday," said Daisy. "Look – there are far more up there today."

The fairies looked at the sky. It was covered with wings, flying all over the place.

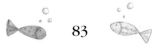

Winnie jumped up and swung her bag on to her back, eager to find out where the wings were coming from. "Come on," she called, "let's go exploring! There's so much we don't know about this island yet, and so many secrets to uncover."

Reluctantly, the other fairies followed Winnie as she led the way from the beach into the mysterious jungle. Hundreds of big-leaved trees blocked out so much light that Winnie had to use a torch to guide the way.

"We'd better stay close together," she called from the front of the line. "Everyone, hold the hand of the fairy in front of you and don't let go."

"I don't like this at all," Daisy whispered into the dark.

"Don't worry, I'm right here," said

Felicity, squeezing her hand tightly.

Then, without warning, Winnie came to a complete stop, the fairies behind crashing into her back.

"Ow!" cried Polly, rubbing her head where it had collided with Winnie's crown.

"Look!" Winnie pointed her torch into the distance. Directly in their path lay a giant mound of earth, big enough to be a mountain. It was glowing with all the colours of the rainbow!

"What's that?" Felicity whispered in wonder.

Winnie, who had no fear, rushed up to the mountain. "It's buzzing," she called out as she pressed her ear to the surface.

"Let's go back, I'm cold," said Daisy from behind Felicity, wrapping her arms around her shoulders and shivering.

"I'm cold too," said Holly, although Felicity knew she really meant that she was a tiny bit scared.

Reluctantly, and after much protest, Winnie pulled herself away from the adventure. She led the fairies expertly back through the dark jungle to their sunny beach, where they spent the afternoon wondering what it was they had discovered.

That night Felicity lay in her tent, sleepily waiting for another rumble, but she didn't hear a thing and soon fell fast asleep. The next morning she awoke fresh and bright from a good night's rest.

* * *

As the days on the island passed,

Winnie explored every nook and cranny of the beach, searching for anything with a rainbow glow. She wasn't going to give up on her adventure, even if the others had.

"This is just the holiday I needed," Felicity said lazily on their second-to-last day. She had almost forgotten about the mysterious night-time noises and the slightly scary discovery in the jungle.

"Me too!" said Holly. "Beach holidays are the best."

That night, though, Felicity was woken up by another low rumble in the ground and a deep buzzing in the air. "Wake up, wake up!" she called out, waking Polly, Winnie, Holly and Daisy instantly.

The minute Winnie woke, she slung

her bag on her back and without a word to the others charged into the jungle!

"Wait for us!" called out Felicity, searching for her flip-flops. "You can't go into the jungle alone!"

Within minutes all four fairy friends – still in their pyjamas! – were trailing quickly after Winnie as she sped ahead. The ground shook more and more the further they went into the jungle.

"Hold on to the trees as you go!" Winnie shouted from the front.

Then, one by one, the fairies started to notice that the jungle was getting lighter, until it was almost as bright as daylight. As they reached the giant mound of earth, the buzzing sound became almost deafening.

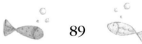

89

"Look!" Holly shouted, pointing her wand to the sky. And there was the most amazing sight any of the fairies had ever seen. A huge ray of rainbow light was pouring out of the top of the mound, illuminating hundreds and hundreds of pairs of beautiful wings.

"So this is how our wings are really made. They're like butterflies, emerging from a giant earth chrysalis," Daisy called, open-mouthed in wonder. "I always knew wings were too magical to be made in boring wing factories."

"Look! Those wings are shaped just like ours!" Felicity gasped, pointing to the ones flying in the direction the fairies had sailed from. "They must be heading for home!"

The fairies sat in awe as thousands

of pairs of wings, all different shapes, colours, sizes and fabrics, danced above the island, saying their farewell. Then the wings flew out above the sea in every direction, to every town in Fairy World.

"That was incredible," Daisy sighed as the last few pairs of wings emerged from the mountain and the buzz faded. "If only we could stay longer."

"Why can't we?" asked Felicity.

"Don't be silly, Felicity, we haven't got enough food for a start and Skipper Sandy's coming to pick us up on the boat tomorrow," Polly reasoned.

Sandy had only dropped the fairies off on the island for a week while she went back to Little Blossoming to get more potion for her on-land-swayitus, a wobbly condition that made her

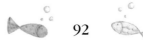

unsteady on land from spending so much time on board a boat.

"I'm sure Sandy's got more food on the boat, and she'll want to see the island too. Oh, let's stay, I'm not ready to go home yet!" Felicity pleaded.

"Neither am I!" Holly called from behind Felicity.

"Nor me!" Daisy agreed.

That night the fairies went to bed dreaming of more nights spent watching the magical wings.

* * *

Right on time, Skipper Sandy arrived bright and early the next morning. "Hello, hello!" she called as she approached the island in a dinghy. Ginny wasn't there – she'd had to leave the boat when they got back

93

to Little Blossoming, to report back to the other wildlife fairies.

"Quick, Sandy's here!" Felicity called to the other fairies. They had each prepared a reason to stay on the island to bombard Sandy with as soon as she arrived.

First, Felicity told the skipper all about the wonderful wing spectacle they'd seen the previous night. "I've never seen anything so amazing in my life!" she started.

"The water is so clear and warm. It's lovely for an early morning swim," Polly followed.

"There are so many parts of the island we haven't discovered yet," said Winnie excitedly.

"And I'm halfway through making a leaf hammock especially for you,"

Daisy continued.

But with enough on-land-swayitus potion to last a week, Sandy didn't need persuading. She'd already planned a holiday on the island with her new fairy friends.

✳ ✳ ✳

"I wonder if the wings will erupt again tonight," Daisy said as they all sat round the campfire after a fun-filled day of swimming, exploring and gathering fruit.

But the wings didn't erupt that

night, or the following night, or the next. On Sandy's fourth day on the island, she told the fairies she only had enough potion for two more days, so they would have to leave then even if they hadn't seen the wings.

"Oh, it's such a shame," Holly said to Sandy, "you would have loved to see the wings erupt. It was truly magical."

However, just as the fairies were getting into their sleeping bags that night, the familiar rumbling sounds began again!

"Yes! This is it!" Felicity screamed excitedly, running into the jungle with the others without a second thought.

Winnie fluttered up to the tallest tree in the jungle for the best view, whilst the other fairies balanced on the lower branches. All six fairies

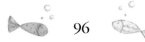

watched in wonder
as the wings fluttered
into the air, stretched,
and hovered close by.
Felicity stretched
her hand into
the illuminated
sky and felt
the trembling
edge of a
beautiful
pair of wings,
identical to
her own.

The magical wings could sense Felicity's kind nature and they trusted her enough to flutter closer to her than any of her fairy friends.

"It's almost as if the wings each have their own personalities!" thought Felicity, as she noticed one pair flip a silly skip in the air, as though it was showing off in front of her.

The fairies sat watching the dancing wings for hours until the last butterfly pair slowly flittered away over the tops of the trees and out to sea. With the magic of nature in their hearts, the friends headed back to camp.

* * *

"Oh no! It's gone!" Sandy cried, waking up Felicity with a start the next morning.

"What's gone?" Felicity asked

sleepily, as she emerged from her tent.

"My potion. I forgot to take it last night and now I can't find it," Sandy explained, swaying as she hovered on the spot. Her on-land-swayitus was setting in.

"Maybe you lost it on the way back from the jungle," Felicity suggested.

"Then I'll never find it again," Sandy sobbed desperately, swaying more and more with each second.

"Don't worry, we'll get you back on board the boat and head home straight away!" said Felicity reassuringly.

Felicity immediately woke the other fairies. They hurriedly packed their belongings and headed on to the boat while Sandy stood on the sand, swaying so much she almost touched the ground with one ear then the other.

"We have to get her to a doctor in Little Blossoming as quickly as we can," burst out Felicity. "Do you think you can remember how to steer the boat, Winnie?"

Winnie frowned, looking disheartened. She hated not being ready for adventure. "It's a much longer voyage than anything I've done before, and Sandy used to stay up all day and all night to steer. I'm not sure that I can do that!"

The fairies all hovered around Sandy, wondering how on earth they would get home. Sandy was too scared to open her mouth in case she was land-sick! She knew that when she had a really serious bout of on-land-swayitus, she couldn't even cure it by getting on to a boat.

"What if we never get home?" Holly cried dramatically.

"Someone will notice we're missing when we don't start school," Polly soothed the others. "They'll send help."

"And in the meantime we can do our best to sail the ship home!" encouraged Felicity.

"But what if we run out of food?" wept Daisy.

In desperation Felicity looked up at the sky, not wanting any of her friends to see the tears in her eyes. Suddenly, something made her forget about their disaster, if only for a second. The cheeky wings that had had performed the silly skip in the air the previous night were dancing for her once again. Dreamily she flew up to fly with them.

"This is no time for playing!" shouted Holly as she saw Felicity disappear into the sky.

But Felicity hadn't heard. She was too busy telling her troubles to the

dozens of
wings that now
surrounded her.

What happened
next was something
none of the friends could
ever have expected in a million
fairy years.

As Felicity helped Holly, Polly, Daisy
and Winnie to lift Skipper Sandy on
to the boat, the sky was suddenly full
of a very low hum. The fairies looked
up and saw the sky was filled with
not dozens, but what seemed like
hundreds of wings heading their way!

One by one, pairs of wings flew
gently into the sails of the boat until

they billowed as fully as they would
have if there had been a strong wind.
And with each full flap the wings
began to lift the boat out of the sea
and into the air!

The fairy friends held on to each
other's hands in awe as the boat flew
through the air, across the clouds

and over the sea towards home.

In what seemed like no time at all, they dropped gently into the harbour they all recognized as home. Immediately, Skipper Sandy was whisked to the doctor's for her potion.

"Thank you!" called Felicity as loudly as she could, as she watched the wings flutter out from under the sails to hover above her head. "Safe journey!" she wished them as they fluttered softly and silently away, pair by pair.

"We'll never forget you!" she cried.

"Or our Wing Island adventure!" she said, turning to the others. And each of them knew it had most definitely been a holiday they would never forget!

Memories are

what make holidays
so special.

Emma Thomson's
felicity Wishes

Felicity comes to Polly's rescue when

she has to perform a lullaby in front of

the Tooth Fairy Agency in

Starlight Songs

Starlight Songs

Felicity Wishes woke with a start, roused from her dream by the clatter of her garden gate and the bang of her letter box. She fluttered to the window just in time to see the Post Fairy fly away in a flurry, looking very tired and weighed down with letters for so early in the morning.

"What could it be?" thought Felicity, who loved to receive letters. "Oh, it could be a letter from Bea. I haven't heard from her in ages!" she said excitedly. Bea was Felicity's pen friend, ever since Felicity had met her on a magical holiday to Petal Mountain.

Felicity flew down the stairs as fast as she could, stopping so quickly she banged the tip of her crown against the front door!

"Oh," she said rather disappointedly as she picked the letter up from her sparkly pink doormat. It wasn't from Bea at all, but had the School of Nine Wishes stamped across the front. Felicity opened the letter, a little puzzled.

"It's not time for an end-of-term report, and sports day isn't for months yet," she thought.

As Felicity read the letter she became more and more down-hearted.

Dear Fairy,

This term you are required to take part in work experience in order to prepare you for Fairy World. You should think carefully before choosing your place of employment and your choice should reflect your ideal future career. If you are unsure of what you wish to be when you leave school you will be allocated a placement that will take into consideration your strengths as a student. Please report to my office in one week, having chosen and contacted your employer.

Good luck!

Fairy Godmother

Felicity's best friends, Holly, Polly, Daisy and Winnie, all knew exactly what they wanted to be after graduating, but Felicity still had no idea. She phoned her fairy friends and arranged to meet them in their favourite café, Sparkles, hoping that they could help her find a fun place to work.

Felicity was the first to arrive at the café and ordered herself an extra-large hot chocolate with a tower of cream on top, dotted with pink marshmallows, to try and raise her drooping wings. She didn't have long to wait before Holly, Polly, Daisy and Winnie came fluttering through the door in a cloud of excitement.

"I phoned them the second I got the letter and they said they'd love to have me after we helped them so much with the newspaper article," Daisy enthused. Felicity guessed that Daisy, who wanted to become a Blossom Fairy, was talking about

Roots 'n' Shoots, the garden centre in Little Blossoming.

"It's just perfect for me – I can look after the flowers and learn more about different varieties while I work. I can't wait!"

As the fairies settled into the chairs around Felicity they were all too excited to notice how unhappy she looked.

"Felicity, guess what?" Winnie beamed. "I called the Land of Pink theme park first thing this morning. They said they would love me to join them for work experience, after I helped them design the park. Isn't that great?"

"Well done, Winne. That's fantastic news," smiled Felicity, feeling very happy for her friend.

"And the Bloomfield Academy for Christmas Tree Fairies said I could join their programme for a week," Holly said, teetering on the edge of her seat, barely able to contain her excitement. "It's going to be so much fun!"

Felicity smiled, truly happy that her friends had found such suitable placements so quickly. Just then Bertie, Felicity's little blue bird, jumped up and down on her shoulder and pointed his beak towards Polly, who was slumped in an armchair, not looking very happy at all.

"Polly, whatever is the matter?" Felicity asked as all four friends noticed Polly's sad face at the same time.

"Well," Polly sniffed, large pearly tears gathering in her eyes, "I phoned the Tooth Fairy Agency this morning and they said they'd love to have me, but I would have to fulfill a simple list of requirements. I thought I knew everything about being a Tooth Fairy, but they've added a new rule."

By now the tears were cascading down Polly's cheeks and making her skirt very wet. Felicity fluttered to her friend's side and put an arm around Polly's shoulders.

"I have to be able to sing a magical lullaby to send people back to sleep if they wake up while I'm gathering teeth," she sobbed.

Felicity smiled. "But you have a beautiful singing voice, Polly; you'll be able to do that easily."

Holly, Daisy and Winnie agreed with Felicity. Polly was the most clever fairy they knew and she could do anything she put her mind to.

"No, I can't," Polly cried. "It has to be sung along to music and I can't play any musical instruments at all. It's hopeless!"

Read the rest of

Emma Thomson's
felicity Wishes

Starlight Songs

to find out if Polly will ever be able

to perform a magical lullaby.

If you enjoyed this book, why not try another of these fantastic story collections?

1

2
Star Surprise

3
Clutter Clean-out

Designer Drama

4
Newspaper Nerves

5
Enchanted Escape

6
Whispering Wishes

Friends Forever

Sensational Secrets

Happy Hobbies

Party Pickle

Wand Wishes

Dancing Dreams

13

Spooky Sleepover

14

Fashion Fiasco

15

Pink Paradise

16

Spectacular Skies

17

Dreamy Daisy

18

Perfect Polly

Winnie's Wonderland

Holly's Hideaway

Fairy Fun

Starlight Songs

Crowning Cure

Fairy Fame

25

26

27

Storytelling Stars

Perfect Ponies

Glittering Giveaways

Look out for these three special editions

Summer Sunshine

Christmas Calamity

Winter Wishes

Felicity Wishes shows you how to create your own sparkling style and make magical treats in this fabulous mini series. With top tips, magic recipes, fairy products and shimmery secrets.

Fashion Magic

Hair Magic

Make-up Magic

Beauty Magic

CELEBRATE THE JOYS OF FRIENDSHIP WITH FELICITY WISHES!

Felicity Wishes always tries her best to make her friends dreams comes true.

Write in and tell us about a friend you think should be praised for her generosity, sense of fun, and kindness, and you could see your letter in one of Felicity Wishes' books.

Please send in your letters, including your name and age with a stamped self-addressed envelope to:

Felicity Wishes Friendship Competition
Hodder Children's Books, 338 Euston Road, London NW1 3BH

Australian readers should write to...
Hachette Children's Books
Level 17/207 Kent Street, Sydney, NSW 2000, Australia

New Zealand readers should write to...
Hachette Children's Books
PO Box 100-749 North Shore Mail Centre, Auckland, New Zealand

Closing date is 31st December 2007

ALL ENTRIES MUST BE SIGNED BY A PARENT OR GUARDIAN
TO BE ELIGIBLE ENTRANTS MUST BE UNDER 13 YEARS

For full terms and conditions visit www.felicitywishes.net/terms

Friends of Felicity

To Felicity

My best friend is Chloe and because she is, she is very funny and always happy. I moved school you see and she was my first ever friend, she was very welcoming and kept talking to me and never left me out or anything. She is very sharing and whenever shes happy I'm happy, shes like my lucky sun :☼: ♡ - ○ - x - ♡

One of my friendship sayings I have is
"Treat your friends the way you'd like to be treated then all will be happy will be friends forever"

Anastasia Chen
age: 10

WOULD YOU LIKE TO BE
'A Friend of Felicity'?

Felicity Wishes has her very own website,
filled with lots of sparkly fairy fun and information
about Felicity Wishes and all her fairy friends.

Just visit:

www.felicitywishes.net

to find out all about
Felicity's books,
sign up to
competitions,
quizzes and
special offers.

And if you want
to show how much
you adore and admire
your friends, you can
even send them a
swish Felicity e-card
for free. It will truly
brighten up their day!

For full terms and conditions visit www.felicitywishes.net/terms